My First Book of
ABC FRIENDS

by Diane Stortz

Illustrated by
Joe Stites

Alligators **a**lways
ask for **a**pples,

Aa

Bb

but **b**ears **b**elieve
bananas are **b**etter.

Cute **c**ats and kittens
can **c**urtsey,

Cc

Dd

but **d**ucks and **d**inosaurs can **d**ance.

Everyone **e**xpects **e**lephants
to **e**at **e**agerly,

Ee

Ff

but **f**oxes are very
finicky about **f**ood.

Gg

Gorillas never grumble
about going golfing,

but **h**ens and **h**ippos
would rather **h**ula **h**oop.

Hh

Insects like to **i**ce skate
on top of **i**gloos,

Ii

Jj

but **j**aguars prefer to
jump rope in the **j**ungle.

Kk

Kangaroos ride in **k**ayaks
and play **k**azoos,

but lizards and lions
are very lazy.

Ll

Mm
Musical mice and **m**oose
like to **m**arch,

but **n**esting **n**ightingales
need to take **n**aps.

Nn

Oo

Otters and **o**rangutans
like **o**ffice work,

but **p**andas **p**refer
to **p**ilot airplanes.

Pp

Qq

Quiet **q**uail
like **q**uilts,

but **raccoons** and **rabbits** are **rambunctious**.

Rr

Salamanders **s**ail the **s**eas in **s**ubmarines,

Ss

Tt

but turtles travel
together on tricycles.

Uu

Unicorns ride **u**nicycles
on the **v**eranda,

Vv

Ww

but whales watch
from wheelbarrows
and eat watermelon.

Xx

Xylophones are played
by Yaks with **yoyos,**

Yy

Zz

but **z**any **Z**ebras
zip up **z**ippers.

For Sallie

DEREK

For Joanna & Lucy

JOHN

Text copyright © 1985 by Derek Hall
Illustrations copyright © 1985 by John Butler
All rights reserved under International and Pan-American Copyright
Conventions. Published in the United States by Alfred A. Knopf, Inc.,
New York. Distributed by Random House, Inc., New York.
Originally published in Great Britain by Walker Books Ltd., London
Manufactured in Italy   10 9 8 7 6 5 4 3 2 1
First American Edition

Library of Congress Cataloging in Publication Data
Hall, Derek, 1930-   Polar bear leaps. (Growing up)
Summary: Baby Polar Bear goes fishing with his mother and learns
that a leap to safety can save his life.
1. Polar bear—Juvenile literature.   2. Animals,
Infancy of—Juvenile literature.   [1. Polar bear.
2. Animals—Infancy]   I. Butler, John, 1952-   ill.
II. Title.   III. Series: Growing up (Alfred A. Knopf)
QL737.C27H35   1985   599.74'446   84-29734
ISBN 0-394-86531-6   ISBN 0-394-96531-0 (lib. bdg.)

Polar Bear Leaps

By Derek Hall

Illustrations by John Butler

Sierra Club / Alfred A. Knopf

San Francisco   New York

Polar Bear is big enough to leave the den where he was born. For the first time he plays outside in the soft snow.

Now it is time to go to the sea for food. Polar Bear's mother is hungry. He rides high on her back, gripping her fur with excitement.

While his mother is busy eating, Polar Bear wanders off. He stands up on his hind legs, as tall as he can, to look out over the Arctic Ocean.

Suddenly the ice breaks!
A small ice floe carries Polar
Bear away from the land, and
he is too young to swim!
He whimpers for his mother.

She roars to her cub in alarm.
Bravely he leaps across the gap
toward her. It is almost too far!
His paws slither on the icy shore.

Just in time his mother grasps him by the neck. She hauls him, dripping wet, from the water. Polar Bear hangs limp and miserable from her strong jaws.

On firm land again, he shakes himself like a dog to dry his fur. His mother wants to find a safe place to sleep. Polar Bear follows her like a shadow.

Now Polar Bear is hungry.
His mother feeds him with her
milk. Then he snuggles up to
her warm body and goes to sleep.